CAITLIN'S HOLIDAY

HELEN V. GRIFFITH

Caitlin's Holiday

illustrated by
Susan Condie Lamb

GREENWILLOW BOOKS, NEW YORK

Library of Congress Cataloging-in-Publication Data

Griffith, Helen V.
    Caitlin's holiday / Helen V. Griffith ;
pictures by Susan Condie Lamb.
          p.   cm.
    Summary : When her new doll comes alive,
Caitlin's delight turns to frustration as
the doll displays a nasty temperament.
ISBN 0-688-09470-8
[1. Dolls—Fiction.]
I. Lamb, Susan Condie, ill.
II. Title.   PZ7.G8823Cai 1990
[Fic]—dc20   89-27228   CIP   AC

Especially for Caitlin

Contents

CAITLIN'S HOLIDAY

The Resale Shop

Afterward Caitlin wondered what had made her do it. She had never taken anything that didn't belong to her. And Jodi had always been her favorite doll. How could she just practically throw her away?

She hadn't planned it. It had just happened. She had been skipping along the sidewalk, carrying Jodi, on her way to Lauren's house. They were going to give perms to their dolls.

She slowed down when she reached the corner where Rigby's Resale was. Mrs. Rigby sold all kinds of things at her store—used things but interesting things. On nice summer days like this, Mrs. Rigby piled some of her stock on tables on the sidewalk in order to attract customers.

Caitlin glanced at the piles of dishes, paintings, and books. She wasn't really looking for anything in particular. She didn't have any money with her, anyway.

Then she saw the doll—the most perfect doll Caitlin had ever seen. She had big violet eyes, a smooth deep tan, and lots of fluffy, gold-silver hair. She was wearing a khaki shirt and shorts and high white boots. A little stereo hung from a strap over her shoulder.

Caitlin stood still, admiring the doll. What was she doing here, lying in a cardboard box among all these cast-off odds and ends? Gently she touched the doll's smooth, cool cheek and her shining cloud of hair.

"You're so beautiful," she whispered.

Caitlin put Jodi on the table and carefully lifted the doll out of the box. That was when she noticed that the carton was filled with doll clothes. Caitlin ran her hand quickly through the box, uncovering sundresses and

The Resale Shop

party dresses, sport clothes and nightclothes. There seemed to be an outfit for every imaginable occasion, along with shoes and belts and jewelry. Caitlin had never seen such an assortment.

"Are these all yours?" she asked incredulously.

Later it seemed funny to Caitlin that she had started right in talking to a doll that way, but at the time she didn't give it a thought. Reluctantly she put the doll back on the pile of clothes and picked up Jodi.

"Good-bye," Caitlin said, and that was when she first felt that the doll was looking at her—not just staring the way a doll stares but really looking at her.

It was an odd sensation to be watched by a doll, and Caitlin had to look away. Everything else seemed normal. She watched an old lady walk up to Mrs. Rigby, who was standing just inside the door of the store.

"I'd like to find a doll for my little granddaughter," the old lady said.

She'll take this one, Caitlin thought.

In a flash she grabbed the doll and dropped Jodi in her place on top of the box of clothes.

Clutching the doll, Caitlin turned and nearly fell over a pile of books.

"Clumsy," a voice hissed from somewhere close by.

Caitlin kept going, expecting to feel a hand on her shoulder any minute. Once she had crossed the street, she gave a quick glance back and saw the old lady rooting through the box of doll clothes. Mrs. Rigby was standing in the doorway talking to her. Neither one was watching Caitlin hurry away.

"I'm hearing things," she told herself.

She tightened her grip on her new doll and ran the rest of the way to Lauren's.

"She Bit Me!"

Caitlin always wondered what would have happened if Jennifer hadn't been at Lauren's house. She thought she probably would have told Lauren what she had done—how she had exchanged Jodi for the new doll before she thought about what she was doing. Then, with Lauren along to give her courage, Caitlin probably would have returned to Rigby's Resale and switched the dolls back again.

But Jennifer was sitting out on the steps with Lauren, and Caitlin knew she couldn't confide in Jennifer. Jennifer wasn't good at keeping secrets, and Caitlin didn't want everyone to know that she had taken a doll from Mrs. Rigby.

Both girls noticed the new doll right away.

"Let me see her," Lauren said, holding out her hands.

Caitlin was surprised at how hard it was for her to hand the doll over to Lauren. She didn't want anyone else to touch her.

"She's beautiful," Lauren exclaimed.

She handled the doll carefully, but Caitlin could hardly keep herself from reaching out and taking her back. It was even harder when Jennifer took her. She didn't have Lauren's gentle touch. Jennifer fingered the khaki shirt and pulled the white boots off and on.

"What's her name?" she asked.

Caitlin hadn't thought about a name yet. "I'm going to call her Nicki," she decided quickly.

Jennifer moved the doll's arms and legs and patted her silver-gold hair.

"Don't mess her up," Caitlin said anxiously.

16

"She Bit Me!"

Jennifer gave Caitlin a disgusted glance. "I'm just looking at her," she said.

Jennifer ran her finger across Nicki's calmly smiling face, and suddenly she let out a yelp and dropped the doll on the step.

"You dope!" Caitlin yelled furiously.

She picked Nicki up and examined her for damage. Jennifer was looking at the doll with a funny expression on her face.

"She bit me!" she said.

"You're stupid, Jennifer," Caitlin snapped. "You're hateful."

She glared at Jennifer, expecting her to yell back the way she usually did. But Jennifer just repeated, "She bit me."

Something in her voice made Caitlin stop yelling. Lauren didn't seem to notice anything odd, though.

"I've never seen a doll that pretty," Lauren said. "Where did you get her?"

"At the sidewalk sale," Caitlin said before she thought.

"At Mrs. Rigby's?" Lauren said excitedly. "Are there any more? Let's go see."

She jumped to her feet.

"No, not at Mrs. Rigby's," Caitlin said quickly.

"At some other sidewalk sale?" Lauren asked, jumping down to the sidewalk. "Come on. Show us."

"I didn't buy her at a sale," Caitlin said.

Lauren and Jennifer looked at her curiously.

"You just said you got that doll at a sidewalk sale," Jennifer said.

"No, I didn't," Caitlin said.

"Yes, you did, Caitlin," Lauren said.

"Well, that's not what I meant," Caitlin said. "I meant I found her on the sidewalk, that's what I meant."

She could see from her friends' expressions that she wasn't being very convincing. But she couldn't let them go to Mrs. Rigby's asking for dolls like the one Caitlin had just bought.

"You won't tell us because you're afraid we'll get dolls just like her," Jennifer said accusingly.

"Caitlin's not like that," Lauren said.

Caitlin was glad to know that Lauren felt that way about her. But when Lauren started talking about putting notices in the local stores to find the real owner of the doll, Caitlin decided to go home before things got more complicated.

"She Bit Me!"

"Bring Jodi tomorrow and we'll do the perms then," Lauren called after her.

"Okay," Caitlin called back.

Then she remembered guiltily that Jodi was now the property of Rigby's Resale.

CHAPTER 3

At Caitlin's House

Caitlin walked down the opposite side of the street on her way home.

This is silly, she told herself. Mrs. Rigby's not going to pop out of the door and scream, "That's my doll."

But she took the opposite side of the street, anyway.

When she got home, she found her mother sitting on the floor, surrounded by boxes and paper bags. Caitlin's

2 0

At Caitlin's House

mother sold cosmetics, and every month when her order came in from the company she worked for, the living room was a mess until the lipsticks and soaps and perfumes and countless other items were sorted and delivered to their purchasers.

"Oh, good," Caitlin's mother greeted her. "You can help me put the orders together before your father comes home and steps on everything."

"In a minute," Caitlin said.

She ran upstairs to put the doll in her room before her mother noticed that it wasn't Jodi. She hadn't thought until this minute that her mother might not like the idea that she had given her doll away. She remembered how she had pestered until she got Jodi.

She wondered if she dared tell her mother how she had exchanged Jodi for the new doll, and then decided that she couldn't risk it. What if her mother made her return the doll?

Caitlin put her new doll in Jodi's old bed and put the little stereo beside her on the floor. She stood for a moment, admiring Nicki's pretty face. As she looked, she had the feeling again that the doll was looking back at her. She had never felt that way with Jodi.

Caitlin turned away from the doll's cool stare and ran downstairs to help her mother sort the cosmetics. It was fun filling paper bags for each individual order. Caitlin's mother said the customer's name, and Caitlin wrote it on a bag. Then her mother read the names of the items ordered, and Caitlin found the compact or eye shadow or hair spray and put it in the bag.

After they had put the filled bags into cartons ready to be delivered, her mother said, "How did the permanent come out?"

"Oh, no good," Caitlin said, taken off-guard.

"That's too bad," her mother said. "So Jodi still has straight hair."

"Well, we didn't do the perms," Caitlin said. "Jennifer was there." She glanced at the clock. "I'm going out and wait for Daddy to get home from work."

Caitlin ran outside and sat on the front steps, watching the rush-hour traffic stream by just across the sidewalk from her. She was unhappy with herself. It seemed that all day she had been telling people things that were not quite lies, but not quite truths, either.

All because of that doll, she thought, but she knew that she really couldn't blame the doll.

At Caitlin's House

There was a parking space right in front of the house. She hoped her father got home before somebody else took it. People often parked there to run into the sub shop across the street, and then her father had to park up the street or even in the next block.

There were usually boys hanging out in front of the sub shop, and she was watching them laughing and punching each other when her father drove up and maneuvered into the parking space. He climbed out of the truck and lifted his big, heavy toolbox out of the back.

"Hi, Daddy," Caitlin called. She ran over and reached up her face for a kiss.

"Careful, I'm dirty," her father said as usual, as he leaned down and kissed her.

He handed her a key and she unlocked the padlock that held the garage doors together. Her father pulled the doors open and put his toolbox on the floor inside. Then he pushed the doors closed and Caitlin locked them together.

As she turned to follow her father into the house, she noticed that one of the boys across the street had stopped his horseplay and was watching her.

I bet he wishes he had a garage, she thought.

Caitlin liked having a garage. It was the only one in the block, on the end of the row of houses. Of course it had been built a long time ago and was too narrow for most cars. The pickup certainly couldn't fit into it, but it was handy for storing things like her father's carpentry tools and Caitlin's bike. She didn't have to keep it on the enclosed porch like Lauren did hers.

"What's new?" her father asked as they walked up the short flight of steps into the house.

"Oh, different things," Caitlin said. "Mom's order came in."

"All put away already, thanks to my helper," Caitlin's mother said.

"You don't get to trip over anything today," Caitlin told him.

"Darn," her father said. "I like crushing lipstick into the rug."

"Maybe next time," Caitlin's mother said with a laugh.

CHAPTER 4

Doll Music

Something was keeping Caitlin awake—a tiny sound like a mosquito buzzing in her ear. She pushed herself up on her elbows and listened hard. It was music. Caitlin's bedroom faced the street, and every night she heard cars go by with their radios blaring. But this was different. It wasn't loud. It went on and on and it was close by.

CAITLIN'S HOLIDAY

Caitlin rolled out of bed and followed the sound. It led her to the corner of the room where the new doll was. Caitlin crouched beside the doll bed and listened. The music seemed to be coming out of Nicki's stereo. Of course, that was impossible.

Caitlin got on her hands and knees and put her ear to the box. It might be impossible, but the music was definitely coming from there. Was it a music box? Caitlin picked up the stereo to look for a key on the bottom. The music stopped.

"Do you mind?" a voice said sharply.

It was the doll. She sat up and glared at Caitlin.

"I was listening to that song," she said.

Caitlin's first impulse was to scream, but she managed to control herself.

This isn't really happening, she told herself. I'm still asleep.

Keeping her eye on the doll, Caitlin backed away until she felt her bed behind her. Then she dropped into the bed and covered herself with the sheet, leaving a little space to peer through.

I don't have to be scared, she thought. This is just an interesting dream. But her heart was pounding.

Doll Music

The doll hopped out of bed and followed Caitlin.

"Give me back my stereo," she demanded.

She looked real. She sounded real. Caitlin leaned over the edge of her bed and looked down at the doll.

"Are you a dream?" she asked.

The doll wasn't interested in conversation.

"Give me my stereo," she repeated impatiently.

Caitlin slid out of bed and sat beside the doll.

"Are you alive, Nicki?" she asked. "Are you a real person?"

"Of course I'm not a person," the doll said. "Did you ever see a twelve-inch-tall person?"

"But you can talk," Caitlin said.

"Look, I feel like listening to music," the doll said. "Can't this keep until tomorrow?"

She took the stereo out of Caitlin's hand and walked in her tiny white boots back to her bed. She sat on the edge of the bed and pulled off the boots and threw them on the floor. When she put the stereo down beside them, it began to play again.

"Will you stop staring?" she asked Caitlin. "Go back to sleep, why don't you?"

"How can I go to sleep when I'm in the same room

with a doll that can walk and talk?" Caitlin asked. "I'm too excited."

"Well, I'm not going to walk and talk any more tonight," the doll said. She snuggled down under the covers and shut her eyes.

Caitlin watched her for a minute and then she got back into bed, although she was sure she wouldn't be able to sleep, partly because she was excited and partly because of the rock music.

"By the way," the doll said, and Caitlin sat up quickly to listen.

"Stop calling me Nicki," the doll said. "My name is Holiday."

◇ CHAPTER 5 ◇

Holiday Complains

"Caitlin. Wake up."

Caitlin heard the voice calling her, but she didn't want to wake up. Her dream was too interesting. It was about being the owner of a doll that could walk and talk all by itself. Caitlin was amazing all her friends. She was on TV.

"Wake up right now."

CAITLIN'S HOLIDAY

It was a tiny voice, but determined. Caitlin opened her eyes, but the dream went on. The doll was standing there, trying to tug the sheet off her bed.

Suddenly Caitlin was completely awake. This wasn't a dream. It was broad daylight and a real live doll was talking to her.

"Get up," Holiday said. "I want to go someplace."

"Okay," Caitlin said happily. "As soon as I get dressed, we'll go over to Lauren's. Wait until she sees you. She won't believe her eyes."

"I don't want to go visiting," Holiday said. "I want to go get my things."

"What things?" Caitlin asked blankly.

"My clothes," Holiday said. "All my beautiful clothes. You left them all behind, remember?"

Caitlin remembered. She also remembered that there were a lot of them. She didn't think she would be able to afford to buy all those clothes.

"There are lots of clothes here," she told Holiday.

"Where?" Holiday asked.

Caitlin got up and pulled several outfits out of her dresser drawer.

"They were my old Jodi's," she said.

Holiday Complains

Holiday looked them over critically.

"I wouldn't be caught dead in these things," she said.

"They're nice clothes," Caitlin said defensively. "Jodi always looked as good as anybody else's doll."

"I'm not Jodi," Holiday said, and to Caitlin's horror she threw herself down on the floor and sobbed.

"I want my things," she cried. "I want my things."

"All right, we'll get your things," Caitlin said hurriedly.

She would have promised anything to stop Holiday from crying.

The whole time Caitlin was dressing, Holiday sat on the floor saying, "There was a sweater with silver stars on it and a jeans skirt that fit just right and a satin robe—I looked beautiful in that satin robe—and a leather coat and—"

"I'm ready," Caitlin said.

"I'm going, too," Holiday announced.

"I'm afraid Mrs. Rigby might recognize you," Caitlin objected. "She might think I stole you."

"Well, you did," Holiday said.

"I did not," Caitlin said indignantly. "I traded Jodi for you."

"Well, then you should have traded Jodi's clothes for my clothes," Holiday said. "I wouldn't dress a dog in these outfits."

Caitlin couldn't help laughing. The thought of a doll-size dog dressed in one of Jodi's little dresses struck her as funny.

Holiday wasn't amused.

"Carry me there in a bag," she said. "Then Mrs. Rigby won't be able to see me. And make peepholes."

"All right," Caitlin agreed. "I'll go downstairs and get a bag, and then I'll come back up and get you."

"Why can't I go down with you?" Holiday asked.

Caitlin tried not to feel irritated. It was wonderful to have a doll that could walk and talk. She shouldn't expect her to be perfect.

"If I take you downstairs," she said patiently, "my mother will see you and wonder where you came from."

"Just tell her you stole me," Holiday suggested.

"Stop saying that," Caitlin said.

"Well, are you going to keep me up here in your room forever?" Holiday asked. "Are you going to carry me around in a paper bag for the rest of your life?"

Caitlin didn't say anything. She hadn't figured out the answer to that question herself yet.

Holiday Complains

"Maybe you should just take me back to the resale shop and leave me there until somebody who can appreciate me comes along," Holiday said spitefully.

Caitlin knew she couldn't do that. As hard to get along with as Holiday was showing herself to be, Caitlin wanted her. She had wanted her even before she knew she was alive, and she wanted her more than ever now.

Downstairs, Caitlin's mother was in the kitchen drinking coffee and reading the paper.

"Hi, want something cooked?" she asked.

"No thanks," Caitlin said. "I'm going out."

Her mother put down the paper.

"Where, so early?" she asked.

Caitlin had forgotten it was early. Rigby's Resale probably wasn't even open yet.

"Nowhere special. Lauren's maybe," she said. "I guess I'll have some cereal."

Her mother went back to her paper, and Caitlin fixed some cereal and ate slowly, wondering if she would ever be able to explain her new doll and Jodi's disappearance to her mother. She didn't like to lie, but she didn't want to tell the truth, either. She realized now that she could have simply asked Mrs. Rigby to hold the doll for her until she got the money. She would be embarrassed to have her mother know how dumb she had been.

Caitlin took a paper lunch bag back upstairs with her.

"What took you so long?" Holiday asked.

"I ate breakfast," Caitlin said. She hesitated. "Do you eat?"

"Don't be silly," Holiday said.

Caitlin took that to mean no. "Are you ready?" she asked.

"I've *been* ready," Holiday said.

Caitlin put her hand around Holiday's tiny waist and gently slid her into the paper bag, although she didn't feel right about doing it. She had to remind herself that Holiday was a doll after all, and dolls were used to being stuffed into bags and boxes and being carried by one leg and all kinds of things that regular people wouldn't like.

"You didn't make any peepholes," Holiday complained in a muffled voice.

Caitlin found a pencil and punched it through the bag several times. Then she checked the contents of her change purse. Four dollars. It didn't seem like very much.

It occurred to Caitlin that if Jodi was still at Mrs. Rigby's, she could buy her back. Why hadn't she thought of that before? Suddenly Caitlin was in a hurry. Somebody might be looking at Jodi right now.

"I may not be able to buy all your clothes today," she told Holiday, "because if Jodi's still there, I'm going to buy her back."

"Well, she can't wear my things," Holiday said.

The Wrong Doll

Rigby's Resale had just opened. Mrs. Rigby was setting up her sidewalk display, but Caitlin didn't see any doll clothes. She went inside and looked around. There was a table full of toys, which Caitlin glanced through quickly and then went over carefully, item by item. There were dolls and doll clothes, but the dolls weren't Jodi and none of the clothes seemed like Holiday's style.

The Wrong Doll

Caitlin moved the paper bag over the table, aiming the peepholes at the tabletop.

"Is anything yours?" she whispered.

"Are you serious?" Holiday asked. "That junk?"

Mrs. Rigby came inside. "Need any help?" she asked.

"I'm looking for a doll," Caitlin said. "And doll clothes."

"Well, that's the right table," Mrs. Rigby said.

"But these aren't what I'm looking for," Caitlin said. "Do you have any more dolls anywhere?"

Mrs. Rigby shook her head. "But I get new things all the time," she said. "New old things." She laughed at her little joke.

"There was a doll out on the sidewalk yesterday," Caitlin said cautiously.

She was afraid she might get herself in trouble by mentioning the doll, but she had to ask.

"Oh, that poor baby," Mrs. Rigby said. "I dropped her, bringing her in yesterday. You wouldn't want her now."

"Yes, I would, Mrs. Rigby," Caitlin said eagerly. "I wanted her yesterday, but I didn't have the money."

"She's in the back room," Mrs. Rigby said, and she

disappeared behind a brown curtain hanging in a door-way at the back of the store.

"Get the clothes, too," Holiday said. "That's why we're here, remember."

Mrs. Rigby pushed aside the curtain and came toward Caitlin carrying a big baby doll. Caitlin had been so sure she would see Jodi that at first she didn't understand that this was the doll Mrs. Rigby was offering her.

"The back of her head is sort of smashed," Mrs. Rigby said, "but a pretty little bonnet will hide the damage. She's a sweet baby."

"Yes, she's sweet," Caitlin said, forcing herself to look at the doll, "but wasn't there another doll? A teenage doll with a lot of clothes?"

"Oh, yes, she went fast," Mrs. Rigby said. "Wasn't that some wardrobe?"

"She's gone?" Caitlin asked faintly.

"She was in perfect condition," Mrs. Rigby said. "Toys like that are snapped up right away."

The bag in Caitlin's hand rattled.

"The clothes, too?" Caitlin asked.

"The same lady bought everything," Mrs. Rigby said. "Don't you want this pretty baby doll?"

The Wrong Doll

"No, but thank you, anyway, Mrs. Rigby," Caitlin said, and she turned to go.

"Come back in a few days," Mrs. Rigby called as Caitlin left the store. "Remember, I get new old things all the time."

◇ CHAPTER 7 ◇

Lauren Just Laughs

Caitlin walked down the block to Lauren's house, fighting disappointment. She was sorry that Jodi was gone, but she did have Holiday, and Holiday was the doll she wanted most. Then she remembered that Holiday had received a disappointment, too.

"Sorry about your things," Caitlin said.

Holiday was silent.

Lauren Just Laughs

"There's no way I can get them back," Caitlin said.

No answer came from the paper bag.

"We'll get you more clothes," Caitlin promised. "You heard what Mrs. Rigby said. She gets new stuff all the time."

A woman waiting for a bus on the corner smiled at Caitlin, and Caitlin stopped talking to the paper bag. She walked faster. All at once she couldn't wait to tell Lauren about Holiday.

Lauren was sitting on her front steps, yawning in the sun.

"Hi, I have something amazing to tell you," Caitlin greeted her.

Lauren stopped in mid-yawn.

"What?" she asked.

"First you have to promise not to tell anybody," Caitlin said.

"Okay," Lauren said.

"I mean, this is a real secret," Caitlin said. "You can't tell anybody. Not your mother, not your brother, not Jennifer, not anybody."

"Okay," Lauren said.

She didn't seem to be taking it seriously enough.

"When I tell you, you're going to want to tell everybody you know," Caitlin said, "but you can't."

"Caitlin," Lauren said patiently, "I know what a secret is."

"But this is an especially secret secret," Caitlin said.

"Are you going to tell me or not?" Lauren asked.

Caitlin was finding it hard to put her amazing news into words.

"You know that doll I found yesterday?" she asked.

Lauren nodded.

"Lauren," Caitlin said dramatically, "that doll is alive."

Lauren frowned. "What do you mean, alive?" she asked.

"I mean alive," Caitlin said. "She can walk and talk just like a person."

Lauren lost interest. "I have a doll like that," she said. "It's batteries."

"This isn't batteries," Caitlin said. "This doll thinks. She doesn't just say the same things over and over. She can dress herself, too."

Lauren raised her eyebrows. "You shouldn't keep it a secret, then," she said. "You could put her on TV and make a million dollars."

Lauren Just Laughs

"*I* wouldn't make a million dollars," Caitlin said. "*She* would."

"Maybe she'd share it with you," Lauren suggested. "Maybe you could become her guardian."

Caitlin saw that Lauren was taking the whole thing as a joke.

"I'm serious about this, Lauren," she said. "And it has to be a secret. If grown-ups found out, they'd take her away from me. They would want to study her and do experiments and I'd never get her back until I was too old to play with her."

"She wasn't alive yesterday," Lauren said skeptically.

"Yes, she was. It just didn't show," Caitlin said. "I didn't find out until after I went to bed."

"You dreamed it, probably," Lauren said.

"I did not dream it," Caitlin said. "Look."

She pulled Holiday out of the bag and stood her up on her knee.

"Why are you carrying your doll in a bag?" Lauren asked.

Caitlin didn't bother to answer. They sat looking at Holiday standing there stiff and glassy-eyed, a fixed smile on her face.

"She doesn't look alive to me," Lauren said.

43

"Holiday," Caitlin said, "this is my friend Lauren."

Lauren giggled. "How do you do, Holiday," she said. "I thought your name was Nicki."

"That's what I was going to call her, but she told me her name is Holiday," Caitlin said.

Lauren laughed again. "Stop it, Caitlin," she said. "She's not alive."

"Maybe the traffic out here makes her nervous," Caitlin said. "Let's go up on your porch."

They ran up the steps and into the enclosed porch and sat on the floor by the window.

"Okay, Holiday, sing and dance for us," Lauren said. "Do a cartwheel."

Holiday didn't do anything, but Lauren rolled over backward, giggling. Lauren giggled a lot, and usually that was one of the things Caitlin liked about her, but today she didn't.

"Please, Holiday," she begged. "Lauren is my oldest friend. If you don't say something, she'll think I made it all up."

"Do a somersault," Lauren said, doing one herself.

"Holiday, please," Caitlin pleaded.

The doll stuck out her tongue.

Lauren Just Laughs

"Look! Look!" Caitlin yelled, but by the time Lauren came out of her somersault, Holiday was just a doll again.

There was a knock on the door and Jennifer burst in.

"Look what I've got," she said excitedly.

She plunked a cardboard box onto the floor and flopped down beside it. The box was full of doll clothes, and on top lay a doll wearing a long black dress covered with tiny black beads.

"Oh, Jennifer," Lauren said. "You've got a new doll, too. And look at all these clothes."

"My grandmother gave them to me," Jennifer said. "I think they're imported, like from New York City or somewhere. You can tell they're very expensive. Look at this sweater. And this ski jacket."

Lauren and Jennifer went through the box, pulling out one article of clothing after another. But Caitlin was looking at the doll. Jennifer and Lauren might not recognize her in that fancy black dress, but Caitlin knew her own doll. It was Jodi, a newly glamorous Jodi. And all those beautiful clothes were Holiday's.

She was afraid to look at Holiday, but it did occur to her that if anything would make the doll come alive in front of other people, it would be seeing those two girls pawing through her wardrobe.

Lauren glanced over at Caitlin. "Aren't these neat things?" she asked.

"Yes," Caitlin said stiffly. She hoped she didn't seem jealous. She wasn't jealous, but she was so surprised to see Jennifer with Jodi that she couldn't seem to behave naturally.

She felt guilty, pretending not to recognize her old doll, but then it couldn't make any difference to Jodi. She was just a doll. She didn't have feelings like Holiday.

"Jennifer," she said, "that doll can never wear all those clothes. Do you want to sell some?"

"No, I don't want to sell anything," Jennifer said. "I love everything."

Caitlin didn't blame her, but it was a disappointment, anyway.

Lauren ran into the house and came back out carrying her doll.

"Can Sandi try some things on?" she asked.

"If you're careful," Jennifer said. "You can try some things on Nicki, too, if you want," she said generously to Caitlin.

Lauren Just Laughs

"Her name is Holiday now," Lauren said. She grabbed Caitlin's doll. "Do you want to try on some pretty clothes, Holiday?" she asked, giggling. "What would you like to try on first? Ouch!"

Jennifer looked up quickly. "Did she bite you?" she asked.

"There must be a pin in her clothes someplace," Lauren said, but Jennifer looked unconvinced. "That doll bites," she said.

"Dolls can't bite," Lauren said. "They can't walk and talk, either," she added with a mischievous glance at Caitlin. She looked as if she wanted to say more, but Caitlin glared her into silence.

They all settled down to the serious business of trying every garment in the box on every doll. Jennifer had just put a tiny blue bikini on her new doll when Lauren said, "That doll looks just like Caitlin's Jodi."

Jennifer bristled. "She's nothing like Jodi," she said. "I told you, this is an expensive, imported doll."

"Don't you think she looks like Jodi?" Lauren appealed to Caitlin.

"Well, sort of," Caitlin said.

"She does not," Jennifer said. "Bring Jodi with you

47

next time we play dolls and you'll see they're nothing alike."

Caitlin picked a flowered dress out of the box and held it up to Holiday.

"I don't have Jodi anymore," she said.

"Oh, Caitlin," Lauren said. "Did you lose her?"

"I gave her away," Caitlin said.

"Gave her away," Lauren repeated, sounding shocked. "I could never give Sandi away."

Caitlin didn't have any answer to make. But she knew she would have given ten dolls away if it meant owning Holiday.

CHAPTER 8

The Blue Bikini

When Caitlin went home at lunchtime, she found her mother in the garage peering into boxes.

"Did you lose something?" Caitlin asked.

"No, I'm just straightening things up," her mother said. "This place gets such a mess." She looked at the paper bag Caitlin was carrying. "What did you buy?" she asked.

"Nothing," Caitlin said. "It's just my doll."

"Since when do you carry Jodi in a bag?" Caitlin's mother asked.

"Mom," Caitlin said. "This isn't Jodi. I traded Jodi for this doll."

She reached inside the bag and pulled out Holiday. Her mother looked surprised, but she was no more surprised to hear the news than Caitlin was at telling it.

Caitlin's mother took the doll and examined it.

"She's beautiful," she said doubtfully, "but I thought you liked Jodi."

"I did like Jodi, Mom," Caitlin said, "but when I saw Holiday, I wanted her so much I just took her."

"You *took* her?" Caitlin's mother repeated, frowning.

Caitlin swallowed hard.

"I was passing Mrs. Rigby's, and this doll was on display out front," she explained. "I traded Jodi for her."

"Oh, it was a trade." Caitlin's mother looked relieved.

"Right," Caitlin said. "Only I didn't tell Mrs. Rigby."

Caitlin's mother opened her mouth to speak, but Caitlin stopped her.

"Don't tell me to take her back. Mrs. Rigby has already sold Jodi." Caitlin didn't want to cry, but she felt

5 0

her eyes fill. "Do you think I'm a crook?" she asked.

"Of course you're not a crook," Caitlin's mother said, ignoring the tears. "But you shouldn't have done it. You could have bought the doll and still kept Jodi."

"I didn't know I was going to take her until I did," Caitlin said. "Some lady was looking at her and I was afraid she would buy her."

"You could have asked Mrs. Rigby to hold her for you," Caitlin's mother said. "You showed very poor judgment, Caitlin."

Her mother's unsympathetic attitude dried Caitlin's tears.

"Anyway, I can't take her back," she said.

Caitlin's mother looked Holiday over. "Well, you haven't cheated Mrs. Rigby as far as value goes," she said.

"She's prettier than Jodi was," Caitlin said.

She wanted to add that she could do things that Jodi couldn't, but nobody was going to believe you had a doll that could walk and talk unless they saw it walk and talk, and Holiday refused to perform.

"She might be prettier," Caitlin's mother said, handing the doll back to Caitlin, "but Jodi was just as well made as this doll. It was an even trade, I suppose. But I still don't like what you did."

Caitlin wasn't exactly proud about what she had done, either, and she was glad when her mother dropped the subject and said, "How about helping me move some of these boxes."

"Okay," Caitlin said. "I'll be right back."

She ran out of the garage and into the house, crumpling the paper bag as she went, but as she started to throw it into the trash bag she noticed that it didn't feel empty. Caitlin put Holiday on the kitchen table and dumped the contents of the bag beside her. It was just two small pieces of blue cloth. Caitlin was about to drop them into the trash along with the paper bag when she suddenly realized that those two little pieces of cloth were the bikini that she had last seen at Lauren's.

"How did this get in here?" she demanded.

Holiday lay stiffly on the table and stared blankly into space. Caitlin caught her up and ran to her bedroom. She dumped the doll and the pieces of cloth on the bed.

"You'd better talk to me," she said. "You stole that bikini, didn't you?"

The Blue Bikini

Holiday sat up with her arms around her knees.

"How could I steal my own bathing suit?" she asked.

Caitlin wasn't going to get into an argument over whose suit it was. There were too many other questions she wanted answered.

"Why wouldn't you talk to Lauren?" she asked. "You heard me tell her you could talk."

"I'm a private person," Holiday said.

"And you bit her, too," Caitlin said.

"I didn't bite her," Holiday said. "I pinched her a tiny pinch, that's all, because she was too rough."

"You have to quit biting and pinching," Caitlin said.

"No I don't," said Holiday.

Caitlin could feel that she wasn't getting anywhere. She decided to drop the subject for the time.

"I have to go down and help my mom," she said.

"Leave me on the windowsill," Holiday ordered. "I need to work on my tan."

Caitlin didn't feel like doing anything for Holiday right then, but it seemed silly to be angry at a doll, so she draped the blanket from Jodi's bed on the windowsill while Holiday slipped into the bikini. Then she put Holiday on the sill.

"I want my stereo, too," Holiday said.

Caitlin set the stereo on the windowsill beside Holiday and left the room without another word.

If I was going to find a talking doll, she thought, why couldn't it have been a *nice* talking doll?

◇ C H A P T E R 9 ◇

On Lauren's Porch

The next morning Caitlin woke up feeling that she hadn't really slept. Holiday had played her stereo far into the night and had sung along with many of the songs. Caitlin hadn't complained. She was tired of complaining about everything Holiday did. But she hadn't slept very well.

She went downstairs and had breakfast with her

mother and then watched a little TV. When she went back upstairs, Holiday was doing aerobics to rock music.

Caitlin pulled out all of Jodi's clothes and spread them on the floor.

"Pick out something to wear," she said, "and we'll go over to Lauren's."

Holiday stopped exercising. "Lauren's again?" she asked.

"She's my best friend," Caitlin said. "We get together almost every day and play with our dolls."

"I need time to myself," Holiday said.

"But you're my doll," Caitlin protested. "We're supposed to have fun together."

"All you want to do is play," Holiday said. "Don't you go to school or work or something?"

"There's no school in the summer," Caitlin said. "And I'm too young to work. I help my mother deliver · her cosmetics orders, that's all."

That comment brought the first gleam of interest Holiday had shown yet.

"Can you get me some makeup?" she asked.

"I guess so," Caitlin said, "but everything would be

too big for you. Even if you could lift a lipstick, when you tried to use it you'd smear up your whole face."

Caitlin laughed at the thought, but Holiday said seriously, "You just get the makeup. I'll figure out how to use it."

"If I do, will you go with me to Lauren's?" Caitlin asked.

She felt that she was learning how to deal with Holiday.

"Shall I wear the blue bikini?" Holiday asked.

"No!" Caitlin shouted, and then she saw that Holiday was making a joke. It was the first time she had shown any sign of a sense of humor.

Maybe she's human after all, Caitlin thought. Well, not human, but humanish.

There was a problem with what Holiday would wear to Lauren's. She refused to put on any of Jodi's clothes.

"They're not that bad," Caitlin said. She was feeling a little insulted because she had chosen most of them herself.

"Yes, they are," Holiday said. "Anyway, they're too big."

"Well, I don't know what you want me to do," Caitlin

said. "You had a chance to pick something out at Mrs. Rigby's, but you didn't like anything."

"I don't want somebody's old cast-off clothes," Holiday said.

"I wear things from there," Caitlin said.

"Well, I don't," Holiday insisted.

Her attitude made Caitlin so mad that she could hardly keep herself from saying "You came from there, remember."

She left the room quickly before Holiday could make her any angrier. Downstairs, she asked her mother for some cosmetic samples.

"I want to try putting makeup on my new doll," she explained.

"Don't get it all over everything," her mother warned, and Caitlin promised to be careful. She only hoped Holiday would be.

Holiday was sulking on her bed and her stereo was blasting when Caitlin ran back upstairs with the makeup.

"Turn that thing down," Caitlin said, and when Holiday saw the cosmetics Caitlin was carrying, she cheerfully complied.

On Lauren's Porch

"Put me on your dressing table, so I can look in the mirror," she ordered.

Caitlin put the makeup on her jewelry box, and Holiday sat there, facing the mirror. The samples were small enough for her to handle and she tried one color after another, applying tiny dabs to her eyelids and lips with her finger, then wiping them off carefully with a tissue.

She finally settled on a violet eye shadow that matched her violet eyes and a plum lipstick that made her teeth gleam white in her tanned face.

She's so beautiful, Caitlin thought. Why can't she be nice?

"Now let's go to Lauren's," Caitlin said.

She half expected an argument. She was getting used to having to talk Holiday into everything, but the new makeup had put her in a cooperative mood. When Caitlin put the doll on the floor, she walked right over to the pile of Jodi's clothes and picked out a shirt and shorts.

"Let's sit on Lauren's steps so I can get some sun on my legs," she said.

While Holiday was dressing, Caitlin slipped the blue

bikini into her pocket. She was going to take it back to Lauren's, but there was no use letting Holiday know before she had to.

On the way to Lauren's, Caitlin rehearsed her plan. She would put the bikini under a chair on the porch or behind a cushion and then pretend to find it.

Lauren met her at the door and they sat on the porch for a while playing Go Fish and eating pretzels until Lauren said, "Let's give our dolls new hairdos."

"Okay," Caitlin said, wondering what Holiday would think of the idea. "Where's Sandi?"

"I'll get her," Lauren said, jumping up, "but I don't call her Sandi anymore. She told me her name is Candi."

Lauren ran into the house giggling. It was obvious that she thought Caitlin's story about Holiday was a joke. Well, that's better than thinking that I was lying or imagining things, Caitlin thought.

Then she remembered the bikini. She pulled it out of her pocket and had started to shove it under the cushion of the wicker rocking chair when she suddenly changed her mind.

This doll has made me almost steal and almost lie,

she thought to herself, but she's not going to turn me into a sneak.

When Lauren came back carrying Sandi, Caitlin handed her the bikini.

"I found it when I got home," she said. "It got in my bag somehow."

"Oh, good," Lauren said. "We looked all over the place for that yesterday."

Caitlin felt sure that Holiday was furious about the bikini. She almost hoped she would be angry enough to show her feelings. She wanted very much for Lauren to see what Holiday could do. But Holiday sat immovable on the floor, her violet-shadowed eyes staring into space and her plum-colored lips frozen in a sweet half smile. Caitlin had a feeling that she wouldn't be very sweet when they got home, though.

"Let's sit out on the steps," she suggested.

Maybe Holiday would be in a better mood if she had a chance to sunbathe.

Holiday Sulks

Caitlin was right about Holiday being mad at her for returning the bikini. She just hadn't realized how furious she would be.

Holiday remained stiff and doll-like all the way home, but Caitlin could feel the anger in her. Her mother was in the kitchen fixing dinner when she got home. Caitlin left Holiday in the living room while she set the table and then sat talking to her mother. When it was time

Holiday Sulks

for her father to get home from work, Caitlin went out and sat on the steps. When he drove up, she helped him put away his tools and then watched TV until it was time to eat. She knew what she was doing. She was avoiding being alone with Holiday.

You shouldn't have to be afraid of your own doll, she thought, but that was almost the way it was.

At bedtime she was tempted to leave Holiday downstairs, but she decided if there was going to be a scene, she might as well get it over with.

As soon as she walked into the bedroom, Holiday started.

"That was my bikini," she said.

Caitlin put Holiday down on Jodi's old bed and sat on her own bed facing her.

"It wasn't yours anymore," she said. "It belonged to whoever bought the box of clothes."

"It's mine," Holiday insisted. "It's not Jodi's. She'll look terrible in it."

"I know she won't look as nice in it as you did," Caitlin said, trying to speak soothingly. "But you could never have worn it. If Lauren or Jennifer ever saw you in it, they would think I had stolen it."

"You did steal it," Holiday said, breaking into angry

sobs. "You stole it and you stole me, and I want my bikini back and all my other things."

She threw herself facedown on the little bed and cried.

Caitlin sat and watched her, resentful and pitying at the same time.

Why does she have to make such a crisis out of everything? she thought.

Caitlin put on her nightgown and got into bed. She lay there listening to Holiday's sniffles and sobs, until after a while the stereo began to play. Caitlin decided the tantrum must be over. She fell asleep listening to the music and wondering if having a talking doll was such a good thing after all.

But the next morning, Caitlin found out that the tantrum wasn't over at all. It had just taken a different form. Holiday lay flat on her back in bed and refused to speak. Caitlin didn't know why it bothered her so much. Jodi had never spoken, and Caitlin hadn't given it a thought. Now, when her doll didn't answer her questions, it hurt her feelings.

If Jodi had been able to talk, Caitlin thought, I bet she never would have treated me like this.

Holiday Sulks

"Would you like to go to Lauren's or Mrs. Rigby's?" she asked into a cold silence. "Would you like to sit on the windowsill in the sun?"

Finally Caitlin gave up and went downstairs for breakfast.

Her mother lowered her newspaper and looked at her.

"Did you and Lauren have a fight yesterday?" she asked.

"Not a real fight," Caitlin said. "I yelled at her when she hid some of the cards when we were playing Go Fish. She always does that. But we weren't really mad."

"You seemed kind of down last night," Caitlin's mother said. "And you still look a little peaked. Maybe you should quit playing your radio at night."

Caitlin started to say "I don't," but then she remembered Holiday's stereo. She would have to tell her to lower the volume. That meant something else to fight about.

Caitlin took an orange and sat out on the front steps to eat it. It usually cheered her up to see the cars flashing past just a few feet from where she was sitting. She liked to watch the neighborhood kids running and roller skating and riding their bikes along the sidewalk. But with Holiday upstairs sulking, all those interesting activities lost their charm. She finally came to a decision. She gathered up the pieces of orange peel and took them to the kitchen to throw them away.

The room was empty. Caitlin looked out the screened door into their tiny backyard. Her mother was out there watering her tomato plants. Caitlin joined her, and together they admired the plants and examined them for insects.

After a few minutes Caitlin asked, "Mom, do you owe me any money?"

"Probably," her mother said. "Why, do you need some?"

"Well, I thought I'd buy some clothes for my new doll," Caitlin said, "but I only have four dollars."

"Don't Jodi's clothes fit her?" Caitlin's mother asked.

"They fit her, but she doesn't like them," Caitlin said. "I mean, I don't like them on her."

"Those outfits are expensive," her mother said.

"I know," Caitlin said. "That's why I need more money."

Her mother thought it over. "Well, I'll give you five

dollars. I probably owe you that much, anyway. But I don't like to see you spend all your money on doll clothes."

"I won't," Caitlin said. But in her heart she had a suspicion that that was just what she would be doing, if Holiday had her way.

At the Mall

Caitlin left her mother counting the tomato blossoms and ran upstairs to her room. Holiday was still lying on her back, showing no more life than Jodi had. Caitlin walked past the doll and picked up her change purse from her dressing table. Then she stood looking down at Holiday.

"I'm going to the store to buy you some new clothes," she said.

Holiday's eyes flew open. She jumped up and

slipped her feet into a pair of Jodi's old sandals.

"I'm going with you," she said, all smiles.

"You'd better not," Caitlin said. "I'm riding my bike."

"I like bikes," Holiday said.

"You'll have to ride in the basket and it'll be bumpy," Caitlin warned her.

"What do I care?" Holiday asked. She laughed excitedly. She certainly didn't act like someone who had spent the night having a temper tantrum.

"How can you go from sad to happy, just like that?" Caitlin asked.

"I don't know," Holiday said without interest. "Let's go."

Caitlin picked up the doll and took her downstairs. Her mother met her in the living room and handed her a five-dollar bill.

"I still don't see why she can't wear Jodi's clothes," she said.

Holiday gave a little snort, just loud enough for Caitlin to hear.

"Thanks," Caitlin said. "I'm going down to the new mall."

She ran out to the kitchen to get the garage key from the counter.

"Bye, Mom," she said as she ran past her and out to the garage.

Caitlin opened the padlock on the garage doors and put the key in her pocket with a tissue stuffed on top of it to hold it in. She got her bike and put Holiday in the wicker basket attached to the handlebars. After she wheeled the bike out to the sidewalk she clicked the padlock shut again and then jumped on her bike and headed for the mall. There was always too much traffic for her to ride in the street, so she rode along the sidewalk, Holiday nearly bouncing out of the basket each time they crossed a crack. Caitlin knew how to make her bike jump down the curb and then back up when she crossed streets, but the first jump almost sent Holiday flying, so she stopped at every intersection and walked her bike across when the light turned green.

The mall was only a few blocks away. It was just a small strip of stores where some old houses had been torn down, but there was a variety store, and that was where Caitlin was headed.

She locked her bike in front of the store and took Holiday out of the basket.

"I told you it would be rough," she said, but Holiday was being a doll and didn't answer.

At the Mall

Caitlin walked into the store and found the toy department. There were piles of little boxes containing a wide variety of doll fashions. When Caitlin saw the prices, she whispered to Holiday, "I only have nine dollars. That's three outfits at the very most."

She stood Holiday on a shelf and held one package after another in front of her. It took a while to show her everything because when anyone came by, Caitlin stopped and pretended to be looking at them herself.

When the fashion show was over, Caitlin looked around to make sure no one was listening and asked, "Which ones do you want?"

"I'm not sure," Holiday said. "Let me see them again. Go slower."

So Caitlin showed her each outfit again. They finally got it down to two piles: a "definitely no" pile and a "possibly yes" pile.

"Are you sure you showed me everything?" Holiday asked.

"Everything we can afford," Caitlin said.

"I want to try some things on," Holiday said.

"You can't try things on," Caitlin objected. "Dolls never try things on. You're lucky you're even getting to pick out the things yourself. Jodi never did."

"Jodi couldn't," Holiday pointed out, and since that was true, Caitlin just started showing her the things in the "possibly yes" pile again. It was nice to see Holiday having a good time for a change, but Caitlin did wish she would make up her mind.

She caught some movement out of the corner of her eye and turned to see a little girl watching them with big round eyes.

"Hi," Caitlin said, and the little girl turned and ran.

"Will you hurry up?" Caitlin said to Holiday.

"I'll take the fur coat, for one thing," Holiday finally decided.

"If you take the fur coat, you can't have anything else," Caitlin said. "That costs all the money I have."

"I want more than one thing," Holiday protested.

"Then choose cheaper things," Caitlin said. "Look, if you take this bikini and this tennis set and this sundress, you'll have three new things instead of one."

"Is three the most I can get?" Holiday asked.

"I've only got nine dollars, remember," Caitlin said.

"I don't know anything about money," Holiday said, "but I want the most things I can have."

Caitlin took that to mean that Holiday would take the

At the Mall

three items. She carried them and Holiday to the checkout counter.

The little girl who had been watching her was waiting with her mother at the next cash register. When she saw Caitlin, she pulled on her mother's arm and stretched up to whisper to her. The woman glanced at Caitlin and gave her daughter an absentminded smile. Caitlin wondered if the little girl was showing her mother the girl who talked to her doll. Maybe she had even seen Holiday herself talk.

Nobody will ever believe her, Caitlin thought, feeling a little sorry for the child. When she gets older, she won't even believe it herself.

◇ CHAPTER 12 ◇

A Fashion Show

Holiday was delighted with her new clothes.

"Sit down on the floor," she said as soon as they were back in Caitlin's room, "and I'll model everything for you."

First she put on the tennis outfit, a white one-piece dress with a short pleated skirt. The set came with tiny pink tennis shoes and a little tennis racket.

A Fashion Show

Holiday served an imaginary ball to an imaginary opponent, and then played through a make-believe set, running and bouncing lightly up and down in her pink tennis shoes, hitting overhead and backhand shots, just like a real tennis player. It seemed a pity to Caitlin that there wasn't anyone her size she could play with.

"Where did you learn to play tennis?" she asked.

"I don't know," Holiday answered. "Close your eyes. I want to surprise you."

Caitlin closed her eyes. When she opened them again, Holiday was in the loose cotton sundress, gliding across the rug like a model. Then, with a quick movement, she pulled the sundress over her head and posed in the new bikini.

Caitlin applauded. "That was a great show," she said.

"Now put me up on the windowsill," Holiday said, "with my pillow and my stereo."

"But I thought we could go to Lauren's," Caitlin said.

"I don't want to go to Lauren's," Holiday said.

"Don't you want to show her your new clothes?" Caitlin asked.

"Some other time," Holiday said. "Right now I want to rest in the sun."

CAITLIN'S HOLIDAY

Caitlin did what Holiday asked. She didn't feel like putting up with another tantrum. She couldn't help feeling resentful, though. Holiday had gotten what she wanted, and now she didn't care at all about what Caitlin wanted.

When Caitlin left the room, Holiday was singing along with her stereo.

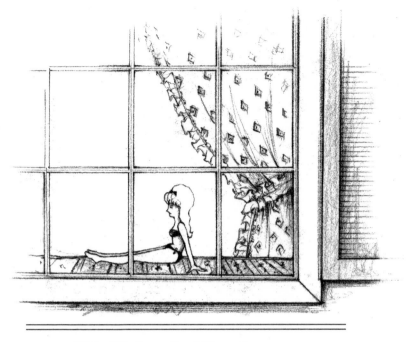

Holiday's Tantrum

Jennifer was at Lauren's, and so was Jodi, looking cute in shorts and an oversize T-shirt from what had been Holiday's box of clothes.

"We're just going for ice-cream cones," Lauren said. "Come on."

They all walked together down to the sub shop across from Caitlin's house. Lauren was carrying Sandi, and

Jennifer had Jodi. She wasn't Jodi anymore, though. Jennifer had named her Wendi. Caitlin couldn't help feeling a little sorry for herself. When Jodi had been her doll, she had taken her everywhere she went. Now she only had a part-time doll.

Caitlin was deciding on a flavor when she remembered she didn't have any money.

"I don't have any extra with me," Lauren said.

"Neither do I," Jennifer said. "Is your mother home? You could run over and ask her for some."

Caitlin didn't like to tell them that she had just gotten five dollars from her mother that morning. She couldn't ask for another dollar already.

"I guess I don't really want any ice cream," she said.

When they came out of the store, Lauren noticed Holiday sitting in Caitlin's bedroom window.

"Hello, Holiday," she called, and she held up Sandi and waved the doll's arm.

"Go get her, Caitlin," Jennifer said. "We can go to my house and play they're rock stars. Wendi came with all kinds of neat clothes we can use."

Caitlin wanted to do it, but what if she went upstairs and Holiday refused to come with her? Of course she could take her, anyway, but then she would have to put up with sulking and tears all night.

"I can't," she told the girls. "I have to go home now."

She walked with them to the stoplight and then crossed the street and went back to her own house. She sat on the steps and watched Lauren and Jennifer walk up the street, talking and laughing together. She felt left out, and it was Holiday's fault. She couldn't even have an ice-cream cone because she had spent all her money on Holiday. She began to wonder why she wanted the doll at all.

When she thought it over, she could hardly remember one minute of fun she had had with Holiday. Holiday hadn't seemed to have much fun, either. She was always flying off the handle about something stupid.

I wouldn't mind as much if I thought she liked me, Caitlin thought, but I don't think she cares about me one bit.

Of course Jodi hadn't cared, either, but that was different. Jodi was just a doll. Holiday was more than that. That should make her more fun instead of less.

Caitlin didn't know what to do with herself. Maybe

she should have gone with Lauren and Jennifer, even if she didn't have a doll to dress up. She didn't feel like seeing Holiday. She hoped she got sunburned from sitting in the window too long. Actually she didn't think the sun did anything to Holiday at all. She was always the same color she had come with from the factory—or wherever she had come from.

After a while Caitlin got up and went into the house. She picked up a book and lay down on the sofa to read it. She read for a long time. It felt good to be involved in somebody else's problem instead of her own. Then her eyelids began to want to close, and she threw down the book and curled up with a pillow over her head to shut out the light.

The next thing she knew, her father was home from work.

"How come no greeter on the steps?" he asked.

"She's been asleep for a couple of hours," Caitlin's mother said. "I think she must be sick."

They both stood looking down at her as she stretched and sat up.

"I'm not exactly sick," Caitlin said.

"Well, what exactly are you?" her mother asked.

Holiday's Tantrum

"Maybe she's exactly hungry," her father said. "What's for dinner?"

"I thought we could go out for chicken," Caitlin's mother said, and Caitlin and her father said, "Yeah."

Caitlin and her mother watched TV while they waited for Caitlin's father to shower and change. Caitlin felt dazed from sleeping so long during the day. She wasn't used to doing that.

She felt a lot better after they had all climbed into the truck and driven through the busy streets to their favorite bright, lively restaurant. By the time they got home again, Caitlin was back to normal and ready to forgive Holiday for spoiling her day.

Her parents wandered up the street to talk to some neighbors who were sitting on their porch, and Caitlin went into the house. She thought Holiday would be glad to get off the windowsill by now. She burst into her bedroom, saying over the noise of the blaring stereo, "It's too bad you don't eat. We had the best fried chicken."

As she approached the window she heard a crunch and looked down to see what she had stepped on. At first she didn't recognize the crushed piece of white plastic she picked up, but Holiday knew what it was right away.

"My boot!" she screamed. "It's ruined. I loved those boots. I'll never find another pair like them."

"It was an accident," Caitlin said. "I'm really sorry."

"I don't care," Holiday shouted. "You should be more careful."

She was so angry that Caitlin started feeling angry back.

"You're the one who left it on the floor," she said.

"That's right, blame me," Holiday cried. "Ruin the one nice thing I have in this world and blame me for it."

Holiday threw herself down on her pillow, pounding her tiny fists and kicking her tiny feet, and suddenly Caitlin had had enough. She snatched the doll up roughly and ran downstairs with her. In the kitchen, she grabbed the key from the counter and then rushed out to the garage. She stuck the key into the padlock, unlocked it, and carried Holiday inside.

Caitlin flung the doll, still clutching her stereo, down on the workbench at the back of the garage. Then she spun around, stalked outside, and slammed the doors behind her. She headed blindly up the street, so upset that she almost didn't hear her parents calling her from the neighbor's porch.

"Where are you off to?" her mother asked.

Caitlin forced her voice to be steady as she answered, "Just around the block."

"I'll go with you," her father offered. "I need to work off some of that chicken."

The walk with her father helped calm Caitlin down. He told her about the house he was working on and how the people who were having it built kept changing their minds about what they wanted. He made it sound very funny, and before they were home again, Caitlin was laughing and feeling a lot more like herself.

"I think I'd like to be a carpenter," she said. "Either that or an architect."

"I'd rather see you open an old folks' home," her father said. "Then your mother and I would have somewhere to go when we get old and rickety."

Caitlin laughed. "You'll never be old and rickety."

"Never?" her father asked.

"Well," Caitlin said, "not to me," and her father gave her a one-armed hug that almost knocked her over.

◇ CHAPTER 14 ◇

Holiday the Hero

Caitlin had some trouble going to sleep that night. She tried to believe it was because she had had a long nap that afternoon, but she finally had to admit to herself that she was worried about Holiday.

Maybe she's scared out there all alone, she thought.

Then she thought, No, nothing scares Holiday.

She worried that the doll might be cold, but then she remembered, Holiday doesn't get cold.

Holiday the Hero

Maybe she's sad because I'm mad at her, she thought, but then she reminded herself, Holiday doesn't care one bit about what I think.

It seemed very quiet in the bedroom without Holiday's stereo thumping away. It seemed lonely, but Caitlin finally dropped off to sleep.

During the night a thought woke her with the shock of a bucket of cold water. She had forgotten to lock the garage doors.

I can't have forgotten, she tried to convince herself. I always lock them.

Caitlin tried hard to remember locking the doors. She went over the scene again and again in her mind. She remembered dropping Holiday and her stereo on the workbench. She remembered walking out of the garage and pushing the doors together. But she couldn't remember squeezing the padlock shut. She couldn't remember putting the key back on the kitchen counter.

Caitlin tried to put the whole thing out of her mind and go back to sleep. She didn't want to go outside and lock the doors in the middle of the night. Her parents wouldn't like her doing that. But they also wouldn't like knowing that she had left the doors unlocked.

After a few minutes of worrying, Caitlin knew she

wouldn't be able to rest until she checked the doors. She slipped out of bed and tiptoed down the stairs. She unlocked the front door as quietly as she could and stepped out onto the porch and unlocked the porch door. It was a warm night and very quiet. The sub shop's lights were out, so it must be late.

It would be funny if I had locked the doors after all, Caitlin was thinking as she ran down the front steps.

Then she saw that the garage doors were not only unlocked, they were ajar. Her heart began an unpleasant thumping. Was someone in there? Had her bike been stolen? Or her father's tools?

No sound came from the garage. Caitlin began to breathe a little easier. Maybe the wind had blown the door open. There wasn't any breeze now, but maybe there had been some earlier.

Caitlin stood there for a long time before she finally risked looking inside the garage. She didn't touch the door, just peered through the narrow opening. Nothing was moving inside the garage.

Suddenly a voice called cheerily, "You can come in. It's safe now."

Caitlin opened the doors wider. The light from the

streetlight across the street shone directly into the garage. It illuminated Holiday, who was jumping up and down on the workbench and waving her arms excitedly.

"Somebody came in here and I scared him away," she yelled. "I really did. I'm a hero."

Caitlin looked around the garage. Her bike was where she had left it. The carpentry tools were there. She grabbed Holiday and ran out of the garage, making sure, even in her hurry, that this time she clicked the padlock shut and took the key with her.

She ran up to the porch, locked the door, and entered the house just as her mother reached the foot of the stairs.

"What's going on?" her mother demanded angrily.

"I remembered I forgot to lock the garage," Caitlin said. "I just locked it."

She showed her mother the key.

"Caitlin," her mother said, still angrily, "don't ever do this again."

"I won't," Caitlin promised in a small voice.

She ducked past her mother to put the key back on the kitchen counter and then scooted up the stairs.

"Good-night," she called softly, and her mother answered, "Good-night." She didn't sound quite as mad.

Caitlin snuggled into bed with Holiday and listened as her mother climbed the stairs and went into her bedroom. When everything was quiet, she whispered, "Now tell me what happened."

"I'm a hero, that's all," Holiday said.

"Well, what did you do?" Caitlin asked.

But Holiday's mood had changed.

"It was no big deal," she said. "I'll tell you tomorrow."

Caitlin knew Holiday wouldn't say any more until she was ready. There was nothing to do but go to sleep.

CHAPTER 15

Holiday Plans

When Caitlin woke up the next morning, Holiday was already dressed in the khaki outfit she had been wearing when Caitlin first saw her. The doll had spread all of Jodi's clothes and her own new things out on the floor and was dividing everything into two piles.

"What are you doing?" Caitlin asked.

"Packing," Holiday said. "I'm taking some of Jodi's clothes. The least horrible ones. It's only fair, since you made me lose all my own things." She examined a seam on one of Jodi's dresses. "Junk," she muttered.

"Why are you packing?" Caitlin asked.

Holiday sat back on her heels and looked up at Caitlin. "Aren't you getting rid of me?" she asked.

Caitlin didn't know what to say. That had been her intention yesterday, but she didn't feel the same today. She scooped the doll up and sat her on the bed in front of her.

"What went on last night?" she asked.

"I told you," Holiday said. "I'm a hero."

"But what did you do?" Caitlin persisted.

"I scared somebody away," Holiday said proudly. "I was busy crying when he came in, but I stopped right away and yelled and scared him off. Doesn't that make me a hero?"

"Don't tell me you cried over that boot all night," Caitlin said.

"I wasn't crying over my boot," Holiday said indignantly. "I was crying because you were mean to me."

Caitlin's jaw dropped. "*I* was mean to *you*," she repeated.

"Yes, you were," Holiday said. "It's boring in the garage."

Holiday Plans

"You're the one who's mean," Caitlin said. "You're always too busy to play with me. And you're always mad about something."

"What's mean about that?" Holiday asked.

Caitlin stared at her. "Don't you know?" she asked.

Holiday gazed back at Caitlin, her violet eyes wide and serious. "How would I know?" she asked.

Caitlin wrapped her arms around her legs and rested her chin on her knees while she studied Holiday. Was it possible that she really didn't know what a disappointment she was?

"I wanted you to be a friend," Caitlin said.

Holiday jumped to her feet. "The way you and Lauren are friends?" she asked.

"Sort of," Caitlin said.

Holiday began bouncing up and down on the bed. "I can do that," she said eagerly. "I can be a friend."

Caitlin eyed the doll doubtfully. "It would be an awfully big change for you," she said.

"I like to try new things," Holiday said, her words coming out in little bursts as she jumped. "And I don't want to live in the garage."

Caitlin had already realized that she couldn't give up Holiday no matter how she acted, but she could see that the doll was afraid she might be sent away. It seemed like a good time to set down some rules for living together.

"If you stay, you'll have to wear clothes from the resale shop," Caitlin said. "I can't afford to buy expensive clothes like the ones you had before."

Holiday was counting how many times she could clap her hands while she was off the ground, but she stopped long enough to say, "Oh, they weren't expensive. I made them."

Caitlin sat up, impressed. "You can sew?" she asked.

"Sure," Holiday said, bouncing again. "I can knit, too. I can do anything." She flopped down on the bed and smiled brightly at Caitlin. "I'll be a good friend to have."

Caitlin still wasn't convinced that Holiday really understood what she was promising.

"You can't bite Jennifer anymore," she said.

Holiday frowned. "Even if she turns me upside down?"

"Well, you can't pinch Lauren," Caitlin said.

"Okay," Holiday promised.

Caitlin remembered another habit of Holiday's that was annoying sometimes.

Holiday Plans

"You'll have to keep your stereo turned down low at night," she said firmly.

"My stereo's out in the garage," Holiday said. "I threw it at that boy last night when I was being a hero. He nearly fainted. His eyes got big and he ran out the door." She laughed delightedly.

Privately Caitlin thought the boy wasn't afraid of being hit with a tiny stereo. It was the sight of a doll coming to life in the middle of the night and jumping up and down and screaming that had terrified him.

"Let's go get your stereo," Caitlin said.

She dressed quickly and ran downstairs, carrying Holiday.

Her mother was on the phone in the kitchen, taking down an order. She waved her pencil in greeting as Caitlin grabbed the garage-door key and ran outside.

Caitlin unlocked the door and walked into the garage. It seemed dark in there after the bright sunlight outside.

"I hope it didn't break," Holiday said. "I threw it pretty hard."

Caitlin walked slowly toward the back of the garage, searching the floor as she went. She felt something under her shoe, and before she could stop, she had stepped on it. She knew right away what had happened, although as she stooped to pick up the pieces she hoped she was wrong.

"Is that my stereo?" Holiday asked.

"I'm sorry," Caitlin said. "I didn't see it."

There was a long pause while Caitlin waited for Holiday to explode.

Finally, in a serious voice, Holiday said, "Caitlin, if your friend stepped on your valuable stereo the day after she stepped on your favorite boot, what would you do?"

"I don't know," Caitlin said. "It's never happened to me."

"It's happened to me," Holiday said.

"I know," Caitlin told her.

"And I'm not yelling or anything," Holiday pointed out.

"You're being very nice," Caitlin said.

Holiday gave Caitlin a dazzling smile. "It's easy," she said.

Caitlin put Holiday and the squashed stereo down on the workbench.

"Where will I ever find another stereo for you?" she said.

Holiday Plans

"Don't worry about the stereo," Holiday said. "Do you know what I'd rather have? A car."

"A car!" Caitlin echoed.

"I saw one at the store," Holiday said excitedly. She spun herself around on the workbench. "It was red and it had a sunroof, and I'm sure it comes equipped with a stereo, so we would be saving money by buying it, wouldn't we?"

"No, we wouldn't," Caitlin said. "Where would you drive a car?"

"Around the bedroom," Holiday said, still spinning. "In the backyard." She shot a glance at Caitlin as she added, "At Lauren's."

"Lauren's!" Caitlin exclaimed. "Does that mean you'd let Lauren know that you're alive?"

Holiday stood still and smiled at Caitlin. "If I had a car," she said.

Caitlin carried Holiday out of the garage and the two of them sat on the front steps in the morning sunshine.

"A car costs money," Caitlin said.

"I can earn money," Holiday said eagerly. "I can make dresses for you to sell. I sew better than anybody."

Caitlin sat with her chin in her hands, considering

the possibilities. It might work. She knew lots of girls who would like to have outfits like the ones that now belonged to her old Jodi.

"All right. We'll try it," Caitlin said finally. "If we earn enough money, we'll buy the car."

Holiday clapped her hands delightedly.

"And after that," she said, "we can buy a piano."

Caitlin looked at the little doll sitting beside her. "Did you say a piano?" she asked.

"I play beautifully," Holiday said. "I'll give you lessons. I'll give Lauren lessons, too. Or would you rather learn modeling? Or gymnastics?"

She smiled up at Caitlin, and Caitlin thought to herself that living with Holiday was going to be fun. A little hectic, maybe. A little expensive. But fun.